Wishing you a Merry

little Christmas and

lots of happy reading

time!

Love,

Mrs. Ettinger

Dear Parent:
Your child's love of reading starts here!

Every child learns to read in a different way and at his or her own speed. Some go back and forth between reading levels and read favorite books again and again. Others read through each level in order. You can help your young reader improve and become more confident by encouraging his or her own interests and abilities. From books your child reads with you to the first books he or she reads alone, there are I Can Read Books for every stage of reading:

SHARED READING
Basic language, word repetition, and whimsical illustrations, ideal for sharing with your emergent reader

BEGINNING READING
Short sentences, familiar words, and simple concepts for children eager to read on their own

READING WITH HELP
Engaging stories, longer sentences, and language play for developing readers

READING ALONE
Complex plots, challenging vocabulary, and high-interest topics for the independent reader

ADVANCED READING
Short paragraphs, chapters, and exciting themes for the perfect bridge to chapter books

I Can Read Books have introduced children to the joy of reading since 1957. Featuring award-winning authors and illustrators and a fabulous cast of beloved characters, I Can Read Books set the standard for beginning readers.

A lifetime of discovery begins with the magical words "I Can Read!"

Visit www.icanread.com for information
on enriching your child's reading experience.

I Can Read Book® is a trademark of HarperCollins Publishers.

Danny and the Dinosaur Mind Their Manners
Copyright © 2019 by The Authors Guild Foundation, Anti-Defamation League Foundation, ORT America, Inc., United Negro College Fund, Inc.
All rights reserved. Manufactured in China.
No part of this book may be used or reproduced in any manner whatsoever without written permission except in the case of brief quotations embodied in critical articles and reviews. For information address HarperCollins Children's Books, a division of HarperCollins Publishers, 195 Broadway, New York, NY 10007.
www.icanread.com

Library of Congress Control Number: 2018952746
ISBN 978-0-06-241057-3 (trade bdg.)—ISBN 978-0-06-241056-6 (pbk.)

Book design by Celeste Knudsen
18 19 20 21 22 SCP 10 9 8 7 6 5 4 3 2 1 ❖ First Edition

I Can Read!
BEGINNING
1
READING

Syd Hoff's

DANNY AND THE DINOSAUR

Mind Their Manners

Written by Bruce Hale

Illustrated in the style of Syd Hoff by Charles Grosvenor

Color by David Cutting

HARPER

An Imprint of HarperCollinsPublishers

One day, Danny and the dinosaur

were walking to the museum

when they saw a brand-new sign.

4

"What does that mean?"
asked the dinosaur.

"A king is a very important person,"
said Danny.

"And he's coming here!"

"Wow, I've never met royalty,"
said the dinosaur.

"What are kings like?"

"Kings are very fancy," said Danny.

"So if we want to meet a king,

we have to be on our best behavior."

"You mean say please and thank you?"
asked the dinosaur.

"Even more than that," said Danny.

"Maybe our manners need work."

"Tell me what to do,"

said the dinosaur.

"I can't wait to meet a king!"

Danny and the dinosaur bowed

to each other.

The dinosaur's bow needed

a little help.

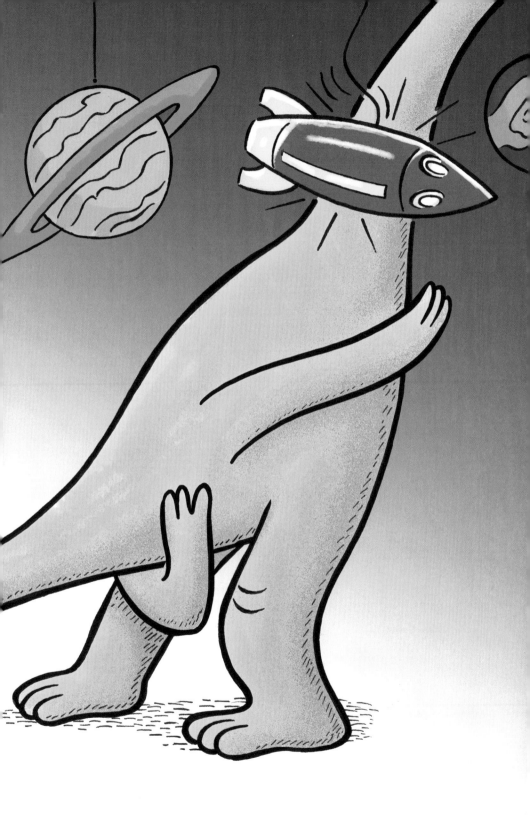

Danny and the dinosaur

tried taking turns

using the drinking fountain.

Danny and the dinosaur worked on
standing up nice and straight.

The dinosaur stood up straighter.

The two pals washed their hands before eating.

At lunch, Danny and the dinosaur
tried eating
with their mouths closed.
It was a little tricky at first,
but they managed.

"It's polite to compliment the cook
after a meal," said the
hot dog seller.

"That was delicious!"
said Danny and the dinosaur
together.

Danny and the dinosaur held the door
open for museum visitors.

"You're so polite," said one lady.

"Thank you, ma'am,"
said the dinosaur.

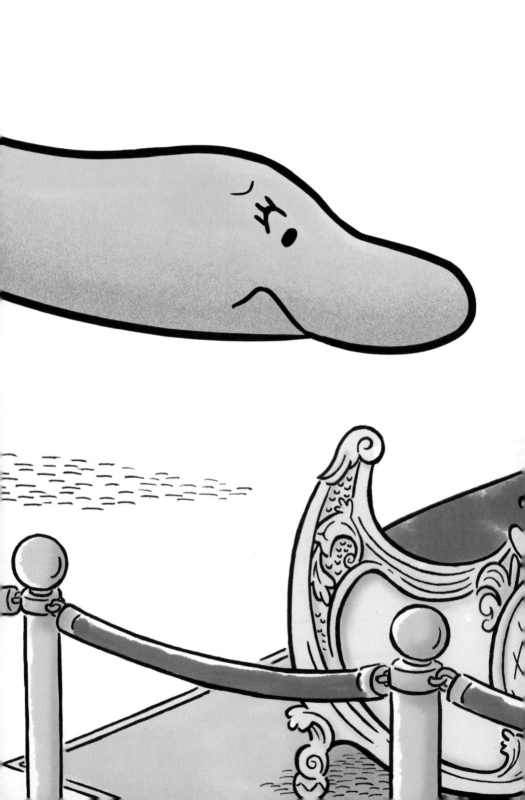

"What do you call a king, anyway?"

the dinosaur asked Danny.

"Mr. King? Your King-ness?"

"Let's ask the museum director,"
Danny said.

"You call him Your Majesty,"
said the museum director.

"Why do you ask?"

"We saw that a king is coming,
and we want to be polite
when we meet him," said Danny.

The director smiled.

"But this king isn't alive.

It's King Tut's mummy.

He died three thousand years ago."

Danny slumped.

The dinosaur looked sad.

All that hard work for nothing?

Then Danny looked up.

"Wait a minute," he said.

"A mummy? That's cool!"

"That's right," said the director.

"And you deserve a reward

for working so hard to be polite."

And when King Tut arrived,
guess who got to be
first in line?